Inky had got a new blue trailer. She could attach it to the back of her tricycle and carry her shopping in it. She could also carry a passenger, she told Snake proudly.

The trailer had a padded seat, and Inky had a cycle helmet for a passenger to wear.

“Shall we go for a ride?” suggested Inky to Snake. Snake nodded. Then he put on the helmet, slithered into the trailer and settled himself onto the seat. “This is nice,” he said. “Let’s go up the hill to the lookout beacon,” he suggested.

“OK,” agreed Inky. “Let’s go!”
Off they went, waving to the other mice they saw at the edge of the village.

Inky pedaled along the lane. As they cycled a bit further, they found themselves by the farm where Bee's hive was. The bees were buzzing about in the orchard by the farm.

"Wow!" shouted Bee when she saw them. "When did you get that trailer? It's terrific!"
"It's new. I got it yesterday," replied Inky proudly.
"Where are you going?" called Bee.

"We're going up to the lookout beacon," replied Snake.
"Fab!" said Bee. "Give me a couple of seconds and I'll fly along with you. I love it up there."

Bee flew back to her hive and told the other bees that she was going out with Inky and Snake.
"Keep a lookout for any patches of heather," said her friend Jazz. "I love heather pollen."
"OK," agreed Bee.

The three friends set off. They stopped once they reached the top of the lookout beacon.
"Look at that," sighed Inky. "You can see for miles from up here. I can see the farm, the village, and the Vowel Forest. The Vowel Forest seems to go on for ever," she continued. Snake and Bee nodded.

They looked at the road running down the steep hill on the other side.
"Shall we go down the other side of the hill, around the back road, and home for tea at the hive?" suggested Bee.
"Sounds good," said Snake. "Tea and cake too, I hope!" he said, licking his lips.

Inky set off down the steep hill. "Wheeeee!" she squealed excitedly, holding tightly onto the handlebars of her tricycle. "I don't even need to pedal!" she squeaked, holding her feet out to the sides.

The tricycle and trailer whizzed down the hill. Inky didn't realize that the tricycle was getting quicker and quicker. Snake held onto the trailer with his tail and shut his eyes.
"We are going too quickly!" he shouted in a scared voice.

"Be careful!" shouted Bee, flying along next to them. "Slow down! There's a corner in a bit, you'll never get around it at that speed!"

Inky tried to slow down. She tugged on the brakes as hard as she could. The wheels screeched, but it was too late. They were at the corner and the tricycle was still going too quickly. Inky tried to turn but she couldn't manage it in time.

The tricycle and trailer missed the corner and crashed!

Inky and the tricycle landed in a tangled heap in the hedge. The trailer unhitched itself, tipped, and slid across the road with Snake still inside it. Bee quickly took out her phone and called for help. Then she went to see how Inky and Snake were.

Snake was lying in the middle of the road.
"Ouch! My tail hurts!" he moaned.
Then Bee went to the hedge and looked at Inky and the crumpled tricycle.

Inky still had both paws holding onto the handlebars but the tricycle was now on top of her!
"Help!" she squeaked. "I cannot get out!"

When Officer Badger arrived, he went to check on Snake first. Snake was now sitting up in the middle of the road, his tail throbbing.

"Ouch!" he cried. "My tail hurts where I landed on it,"

"Hold on," said Officer Badger. "The ambulance is on its way, I can hear the sirens."

The ambulance arrived with Doctor West, the hedgehog. She jumped out and went across to Snake. She checked him over, and then helped him into the back of the ambulance. Snake lay on the stretcher and Doctor West carefully arranged his tail to keep it straight.

Meanwhile, Officer Badger had lifted the tricycle off Inky. Doctor West hurried over to examine Inky and check she was OK. One of Inky's arms was at a strange angle, so Doctor West bandaged it to keep it still. She carefully helped Inky to the ambulance, strapped her in, and gave her some medicine to help with the pain.

Bee waited and explained to Officer Badger what had happened.

At the hospital, Doctor West examined both Snake and Inky again and took some x-rays.
"You are very lucky," she said to Snake. "You have some scrapes and scratches, but otherwise you are fine. It was a good job you had a cycle helmet on, otherwise you would have had more damage to your head."

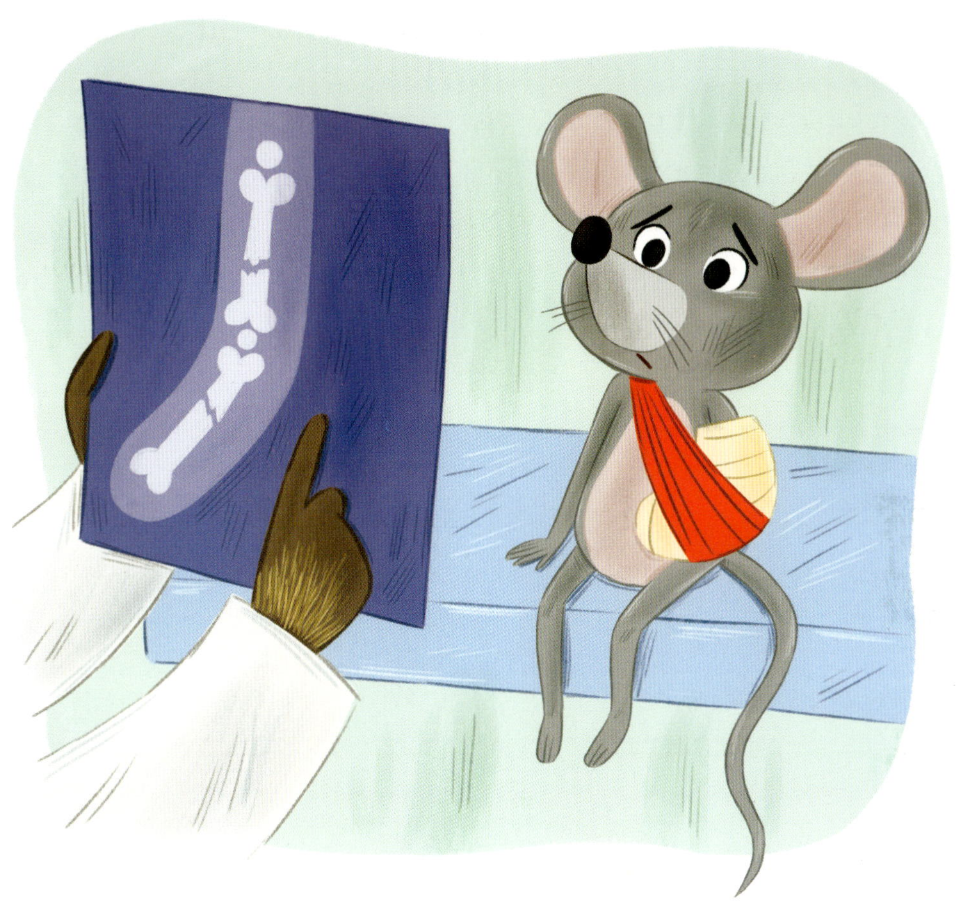

Then Doctor West turned to Inky.
"You have some deep scratches on your face from where you landed in the hedge, but they will soon heal," he said. "Looking at your x-ray, you have also broken your arm," she continued. "We'll get it sorted out and put it in a sling. It will take about six weeks to heal, so there will be no more tricycle riding until then."

"You should be more careful, Inky," said Doctor West. "Don't go racing downhill on any bike, let alone a bike with a trailer on the back," she scolded.

Inky nodded. "I have learned my lesson," she said. "I will be much more careful. We were having such a good time until we crashed," she said, sadly. "I just hope my tricycle and trailer can be fixed, as well as my arm!"